THIS WALKER BOOK BELONGS TO:

For Fergus Robert

First published 1986 by Walker Books Ltd
87 Vauxhall Walk, London SE11 5HJ

This edition published 2001

2 4 6 8 10 9 7 5 3 1

© 1986 Shirley Hughes

This book has been typeset in Vendome

Printed in Hong Kong

All rights reserved

British Library Cataloguing in Publication Data:
a catalogue record for this book
is available from the British Library

ISBN 0-7445-6984-2

Two Shoes, New Shoes

Shirley Hughes

WALKER BOOKS
AND SUBSIDIARIES
LONDON • BOSTON • SYDNEY

Two shoes, new shoes,
Bright shiny blue shoes.

High-heeled ladies' shoes,
For standing tall,

Button-up baby's shoes,
Soft and small.

Slippers, warm by the fire,

Lace-ups in the street.

Gloves are for hands

And socks are for feet.

A crown in a cracker,

A hat with a feather,

Sun hats,

Fun hats,

Hats for bad weather.

A clean white T-shirt laid on the bed,

Two holes for arms ...

And one for the head.

Zip up a zipper, button a coat,

A shoe for a bed, a hat for a boat.

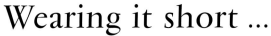 Wearing it short ...

And wearing it long,

Getting it right ...

And getting it wrong.

Trailing finery,
Dressed for a ball,

And into the bath

Wearing nothing at all!

WALKER BOOKS

The Nursery Collection

SHIRLEY HUGHES says that she found working on The Nursery Collection "very stimulating". They were her first books for very young children and she remarks that creating them was "concentrated and exhausting because it was like actually being with a very small child." The brother and sister featured in the books reappear in her book of seasonal verse *Out and About* and in a series of books about "doing words" – *Bouncing*, *Chatting*, *Giving* and *Hiding* – now collected in a single volume as *Let's Join In*.

Shirley Hughes has won numerous awards, including the Kate Greenaway Medal for *Dogger* and the Eleanor Farjeon Award for services to children's literature. In 1999 she was awarded the OBE. Among her many popular books are the *Alfie and Annie Rose*, *Lucy and Tom* and *Tales of Trotter Street* series.

Shirley and her husband, a retired architect, have lived in the same house in west London for more than forty years. They have three grown-up children and six grandchildren.

ISBN 0-7445-6983-4 (pb)   ISBN 0-7445-6986-9 (pb)   ISBN 0-7445-6984-2 (pb)   ISBN 0-7445-6981-8 (pb)   ISBN 0-7445-6985-0 (pb)   ISBN 0-7445-6982-6 (pb)